S0-ALJ-522

ANCIENT AMERICA

BY JIM OLLHOFF

VISIT US AT
WWW.ABDOPUBLISHING.COM

Published by ABDO Publishing Company, 8000 West 78th Street, Suite 310, Edina, MN 55439. Copyright ©2012 by Abdo Consulting Group, Inc. International copyrights reserved in all countries. No part of this book may be reproduced in any form without written permission from the publisher. ABDO & Daughters™ is a trademark and logo of ABDO Publishing Company.

Printed in the United States of America, North Mankato, Minnesota.
042011
092011

 PRINTED ON RECYCLED PAPER

Editor: John Hamilton
Graphic Design: Sue Hamilton
Cover Design: Neil Klinepier
Cover Photo: National Geographic
Interior Photos and Illustrations: AP-pgs 12, 26 & 27; Corbis-pgs 18 & 29; Getty Images-pgs 8, 9 & 22; Granger Collection-pgs 19 & 28; National Geographic-pgs 13, 14, 15, 16, 17, 20, 21, 23, 24 & 25; ThinkStock-pgs 4, 5, 7, 10, 11 & 32; United States Government-pg 6.

Library of Congress Cataloging-in-Publication Data

Ollhoff, Jim, 1959-
   Ancient America / Jim Ollhoff.
      p. cm. -- (Hispanic American history)
   Includes index.
   ISBN 978-1-61783-052-5
   1. Indian--History. 2. Latin America--History. 3. Latin America--Antiquities. I. Title.
   E65.O45 2012
   980'.01--dc22
                          2011012078

CONTENTS

WHAT'S IN A NAME?

What do you call people who come from Central and South America?

There is no answer to that question that satisfies everyone.

In the early 1900s, Spanish-speaking people who lived in the United States wanted the government to acknowledge them. Laws were sometimes passed that discriminated against Spanish-speaking people, and they knew it would be easier to identify those laws if they were an acknowledged group. So, the word "Hispanic" was born. It came from the Spanish name for Spain, meaning "those who are descended from Spanish immigrants."

In the United States Census, people are asked to identify their race. The word "race" usually means "skin color," such as white or black. The census used to include Hispanic as a race. However, that didn't really work because Hispanic people can be of any skin color. The census now has a section for "ethnicity," which refers to a person's culture, not skin color.

Another problem with the term Hispanic was that there were hundreds of thousands of Indians in Central and South America who were suddenly described as Hispanic. But these people were not descended from Spanish immigrants.

Historically, the term "Hispanic" meant people who descended from Spanish immigrants. Today, it is a term that refers to a person's culture.

5

Many people from Central and South America had both Spanish and Indian heritage. Many had African ancestors as well, since millions of Africans were brought there as slaves, beginning in the early 1500s.

To make things more complicated, not all of Central and South America was settled by the Spanish. Brazil was settled by the Portuguese. Are they Hispanic? Some say yes, some say no. Some islands in the Caribbean were settled by the French. Some countries in South America were settled by the Dutch. So, names and labels can be very confusing.

The word "Latino" is another popular term. It is used by many Spanish-speaking people and organizations to describe themselves. "Latino" comes from the word "Latin," the ancient language on which Spanish is based.

Some people prefer the term Latino. Some prefer the word Hispanic. Some people use more specific terms and identify the country of their most recent ancestors, such as "Mexican-American" or "Colombian-American."

Many people don't like these kinds of labels at all. They simply prefer the term "American."

Because Americans who came from Central and South America have very different heritages, the United States 2010 Census asked for more specific information.

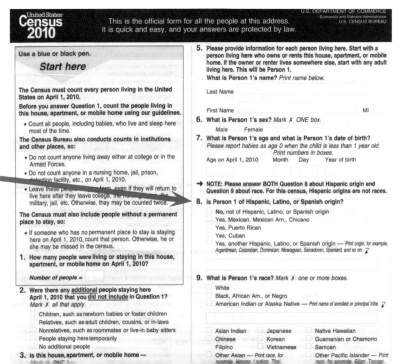

Today, some people use terms that identify the country of their most recent ancestors, such as Mexican-American.

BECOMING HISPANIC

How does a person become "Hispanic"? The United States government officially recognizes about 20 countries and territories as Hispanic. These countries and territories are usually recognized as Argentina, Bolivia, Chile, Colombia, Costa Rica, Cuba, Dominican Republic, Ecuador, El Salvador, Guatemala, Honduras, Mexico, Nicaragua, Panama, Paraguay, Peru, Puerto Rico, Spain, Uruguay, and Venezuela. However, anyone who wants to identify himself or herself as Hispanic is allowed to do so.

Sometimes, people think of Hispanic as "people who speak Spanish as their first language." However, sometimes people who don't know the Spanish language consider themselves Hispanic. People from Brazil are sometimes considered to be Hispanic, even though most Brazilians are of Portuguese descent, and the official language is Portuguese.

In the 1500s, explorers and conquerors from Spain, called conquistadors, came to the Americas. At first, they were looking for a route to India and China. Then, they began to look for gold and other treasures that they could take back to Spain. Later, they began to settle the Americas. Spanish colonists intermarried with the native peoples. Ancient America was already full of native peoples when the Spanish arrived. Advanced civilizations like the Maya, Aztecs, and Inca had been living in Central and South America for thousands of years.

POPULATING THE AMERICAS

Scientists believe that humanity evolved in the eastern side of Africa. About 50,000 years ago, modern humans started spreading out across the world. Some went north to Europe, others went to other parts of Africa. Others went east, toward Asia. People began to settle in every area of Africa, Europe, and Asia.

Long ago, when sea levels were lower, people crossed a land bridge in what is today a waterway called the Bering Strait.

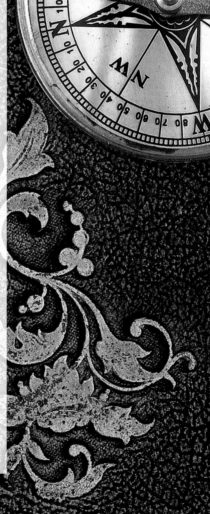

Sometime between 25,000 and 12,000 years ago, Asian peoples moved farther east toward North America. In those days, a huge amount of water was frozen in giant glaciers that covered large parts of the northern continents. Sea levels were much lower than today. This opened up dry land between Asia and North America, through what is today a waterway called the Bering Strait. People walked across this land, probably hunting herds of animals. These people became known as Paleo-Indians. They were the ancestors of the Native Americans on the North and South American continents. These Paleo-Indians spread out to every part of North and South America.

The *Mata Rangi II* was a 95-foot (29-m) -long reed boat built using traditional materials and techniques. In 1999, mariners sailed it across the Pacific Ocean. The trip proved that ancient peoples could have traveled across the oceans.

Most scientists also think that people came to the Americas in other ways, too. Some came by boats from Asia and the South Pacific Ocean. Others may have come across the Atlantic Ocean. It is more difficult to find evidence for these ideas, but many scientists are convinced that people came to the Americas in a variety of ways.

People settled in all parts of North, Central, and South America. They developed their own cultures and their own religions. They formed villages and towns, and developed trading routes. Often, they waged war against their neighbors.

The Maya city of Aguateca was destroyed by native invaders in the 8th century AD.

13

SETTLERS OF MEXICO: THE MAYA

Many thousands of people lived in Central America in family groups, villages, towns, and city-states. Perhaps beginning about 200 AD, groups of people living in the present day areas of Mexico and the Yucatán Peninsula began to form a loose association. They called themselves the Maya. This group of kingdoms and tribes was made up of many city-states and many languages.

The Maya built huge temples, pyramids, and stone sculptures. They had an advanced understanding of astronomy and mathematics. They wrote thousands of books, but unfortunately, most of those books have been lost. From 250 AD to 900 AD, the Maya built large cities and their empire flourished. They traded goods with far-away cultures.

The Maya were excellent weavers, stone workers, and scientists.

One of the most famous Maya cities is Chichen Itza. The ruins of the city are still standing today in southern Mexico's Yucatán Peninsula. The city ruins contain magnificent temples, steam baths, and many other buildings.

About 900 AD, the Maya civilization began to quickly decline. Cities were abandoned, and building projects stopped. People migrated to other areas and joined other tribes. Some Maya cities lasted for a few hundred more years, but the great civilization of the Maya was over.

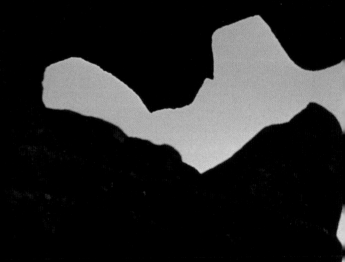

A stone snake head on a nearby temple overlooks El Castillo.

Historians aren't sure exactly why the Maya civilization collapsed. It was probably a combination of several things. The Maya were likely weakened by constant warfare. They may have over-farmed and over-hunted, leaving small food supplies that couldn't feed their huge cities. There is also evidence of a decades-long drought.

The lack of rain may have dried up the crops, making the food supply even smaller.

There are about seven million people today who claim to be descended from the Maya. Most of them live in Southern Mexico, Guatemala, Belize, and Honduras. Many of them have tried to retain some of the culture of their ancestors.

In the city of Chichen Itza stands the Temple of Kukulcan, a feathered serpent god of the Maya. Kukulcan was closely related to the Aztec god Quetzalcoatl. The 75-foot (23-m) pyramid is also called El Castillo, which is Spanish for "the castle."

SETTLERS OF MEXICO: THE AZTECS

A few hundred years after the Maya civilization collapsed, another group of people began to emerge. These peoples founded the city of Tenochtitlán about 1325 AD, and this became the capital of the Aztec Empire. Some historians date the start of the Aztec Empire to 1427, with the merger of three large city-states. This alliance of city-states became known as the Aztecs, a very powerful empire. Today, the ruins of Tenochtitlán are located in Mexico City.

Montezuma, the Aztec emperor.

*A model of the Great Temple
at Tenochtitlán.*

19

The Aztecs were expert farmers, cultivating many crops with complex irrigation systems. They were artists, and created beautiful crafts. Their clothing and paintings were richly colored. Many objects, from the emperor's headdress to ceremonial knives, were encrusted with precious stones and jewels.

The Aztecs built a huge empire, largely through their military might. By 1500 AD, there may have been as many as six million people in the Aztec Empire.

The Aztecs were perhaps most famous for their practice of human sacrifice. They sacrificed people, usually conquered enemies, to their gods. These bloody rituals killed thousands of people every year. The Aztecs believed the sacrifices would calm their angry gods.

The Aztec Empire came to an abrupt end in 1521, two years after a group of Spanish soldiers, led by Hernán Cortés, invaded the Aztec lands. The Spanish brought with them a weapon they didn't even realize they had: smallpox.

Historians say that it's possible that up to half the Aztec population contracted the dreaded and often-fatal disease. The Aztecs had no immunity to this disease, and no idea how to treat it.

The Aztecs fought the Spanish, but the conquistadors had horses and superior weapons.

The Spanish also had better military technology. The Spanish had guns, and they had swords made of steel, which were much harder than the weapons of the Aztecs. They had horses, which the Aztecs had never before seen. With the help of local Indian tribes who were enemies of the Aztecs, the Spanish smashed Tenochtitlán. The Aztec civilization collapsed.

SETTLERS OF PERU: THE INCA

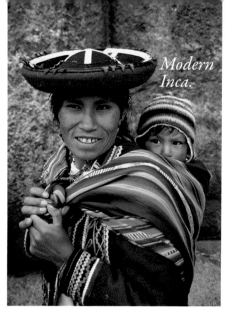

Modern Inca.

People had lived in the western side of South America for thousands of years. Family groups became villages, and villages grew into towns. Then, in about 1200 AD, a new people emerged. They were called the Inca, and they were a powerful and creative people. They liked to live in the high areas of the Andes Mountains. They made their capital at a city called Cusco, which today is in the nation of Peru. The Inca expanded their empire by conquering tribes and nations around them. By the 1400s, their empire stretched across most of the west side of South America.

The Inca were great builders. They are famous for their walls, composed of giant, irregularly shaped blocks that fit together perfectly. The walls used no mortar, and yet the blocks were carved so carefully that even a knife blade couldn't fit between them. The Inca builders would repeatedly lower a giant block onto another, and then hammer away at the sides of the blocks until they fit together perfectly. It was a time-consuming process, but it made the walls very strong. Many of the walls stand to this day.

An annual dance performed in Cusco's Holy Square.

Machu Picchu, the lost city of the Inca, was found by American explorer Hiram Bingham in 1911.

Perhaps the most famous Inca city is Machu Picchu. Built high in the mountains, it was settled about 1450, and mostly abandoned about a century later. It was re-discovered in 1911, and is sometimes referred to as "the lost city of the Inca."

Because many of the Inca lived in the mountains, they had to find a way to grow crops on steep inclines. They developed terraces, narrow level ground that they cut into the side of the mountains.

Spanish conquistadors entered the area in 1526. They knew the Inca had a civilization of great power and wealth. Within the next few years, the Inca were weakened by internal conflict and civil war.

The Spanish were able to find many other Indian tribes to go to war against the Inca. Also, like the Aztecs, they were decimated by smallpox. So, in 1532, the Inca civilization collapsed at the hands of the conquistadors.

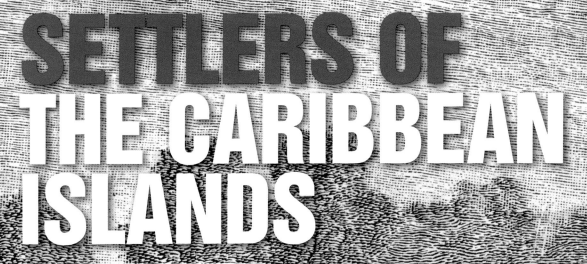

SETTLERS OF THE CARIBBEAN ISLANDS

The Caribbean Sea is an area of water between the southeast United States and South America. It is bordered by Mexico on the west side and the Atlantic Ocean to the east. Strings of islands—hundreds of them— litter the Caribbean Sea. Christopher Columbus landed on one of these islands in 1492.

Even before Columbus, the islands were filled with villages, towns, and Indian nations. The two main Indian nations were the Arawak and the Carib. The Indian nations left no written records, so historians have to rely on Spanish descriptions of them.

The Spanish said that the Arawak were a peaceful people, and that the Carib were more warlike.

Most of the people lived near the coast, where they could easily fish for food. When the Spanish arrived in the late 1490s and early 1500s, it didn't take very long for the meetings to become battles. The Spanish conquered the Indian peoples, and enslaved many of them.

In 1492, Columbus was welcomed by Guacanagari, one of the five native chiefs of today's Haiti.

THE AMERICAS IN THE 1400s

The Americas were a crowded place when Columbus arrived in 1492. There were probably more people living in the Americas than were living in Europe. Thousands of villages, towns, and cities were scattered all over the Americas.

The Spanish came to the Caribbean islands in the late 1490s, and to the mainland of the Americas in the early 1500s. It only took a few years for them to settle all across the Caribbean, Central and South America, and even parts of Florida.

The meetings of the Spanish and Indian peoples were often bloody clashes. The conquistadors led small armies to conquer vast areas. The Spanish invasion was helped by European germs like smallpox, which killed many more Indians than Spanish swords.

The Spanish settlers intermarried with people from the Indian nations. Today, most people from Mexico and much of South America are descended from both Spanish settlers and the Indian peoples.

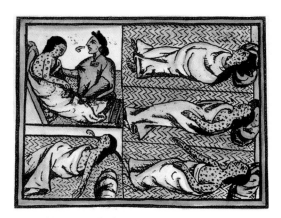

Smallpox killed vast numbers of natives.

In the 1400s and 1500s, the Spanish conquered many native tribes in the Americas, including the Zuni people of today's New Mexico.

29

GLOSSARY

ANCESTORS

The people from whom a person is directly descended. This term usually refers to people in generations prior to a person's grandparents.

AZTEC

A powerful civilization in southern Mexico, emerging in the 1300s. Aztec civilization came to an end in 1521 at the hands of Spanish conquistadors.

BERING STRAIT

The waterway that divides Siberia, a vast area of central and eastern Russia, from Alaska. It was discovered by Vitus Bering in 1728.

CENSUS

A government's records that show information about who lives in a country and where they live. Also, the process of collecting that information.

CITY-STATE

A major city, together with the area that surrounds it, that forms its own independent state.

CONQUISTADORS

Spanish military men who explored the New World and conquered many of the Indian tribes living in the Americas.

HERNÁN CORTÉS

A Spanish conquistador (1485–1547) who led his troops and conquered the Aztec Empire in 1519-1521.

IMMIGRANT

A person who has entered a country intending to live there permanently.

INCA

A civilization on the west side of South America. They emerged in the 1200s and were conquered by the Spanish in the 1530s.

MACHU PICCHU

A city of the Inca, abandoned in the 1500s and rediscovered in 1911.

MAYA

A civilization in Central America that existed from about 200 AD to about 900 AD.

MIGRATE

When a group of people move from one place to another.

MONTEZUMA II

The last emperor of the Aztecs who lived from 1466-1520. He and his people were conquered by the Spanish in 1519-1521.

PALEO-INDIANS

Considered to be the first residents of North and South America. They came across the Bering Strait from Asia at least 12,000 years ago.

QUETZALCOATL

The Aztec creator god. He is often pictured as a feathered serpent.

SMALLPOX

An often-deadly disease unknowingly brought by the Spanish. The peoples of the Americas had no immunity to the disease, so it spread like wildfire throughout the American populations.

INDEX

Quetzalcoatl